The tunnel web of the
Ciniflonidae species

Cradle web of the Linyphiidae
species

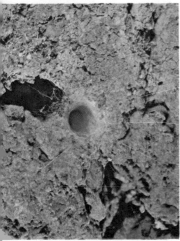

Web of Atypidaes, the British
relative of the Trap-door spider

Spider's egg cocoon in gorse

For some people the word spiders *sends shudders down the spine. Spiders are associated with dusty rooms filled with cobwebs hanging from the ceilings.*

In fact spiders are well worth getting to know. They lead fascinating lives and help Man by eating disease-spreading insects.

This book gives an introduction to the many kinds of spiders found around the world. The colour illustrations and photographs enhance the description of spiders' habitats, life cycles and web-making activities which are all part of The Story of the Spider.

Acknowledgments:
The publishers would like to thank Dorothy Paull for her assistance in the preparation of this book.
The photograph on page 46 is by kind permission of Seaphot and that on page 47 by Popperfoto.
The cover photograph is by kind permission of Oxford Scientific Films.

© LADYBIRD BOOKS LTD MCMLXXX

The story of the
Spider

written by JOHN PAULL
illustrated by PAT OAKLEY, HURLSTON DESIGN LTD
photographs by MICHAEL WHITEHEAD

Ladybird Books Loughborough

Pallas Athene and Arachne

Spiders are *Arachnids* and people who study the spider family are called *Arachnologists*. The word *Arachne* is from the Greek Language and means spider. There is a Greek myth about a woman called Arachne.

Arachne spent all her time making the most exquisite tapestries and boasting that nobody in the world could make anything as beautiful. She thought she was so good that she challenged the goddess Pallas Athene to see who could make the most breathtaking tapestry.

Arachne worked at her tapestry harder than she had ever worked before. When she had finished her work of art she showed it to Athene. It was obvious to everyone that Arachne's beautiful tapestry was better than the one made by Athene.

The goddess was so angry that she tore it to pieces. Arachne was very upset. She worried so much and became so depressed that eventually she hanged herself.

The goddess Athene felt sorry and sad that this had happened. She changed Arachne into a spider so that she could continue making the beautiful tapestries that we see all over our gardens — spiders' webs.

Argiope bruennichi (14mm)

5

What are spiders?

Spiders are fascinating and surprising creatures, quite different from the hordes of insects that live around us. Spiders are called Arachnids, belonging to a class of creatures which includes scorpions and mites. The difference between spiders and insects is easy to see with the naked eye. Insects, such as beetles and ants, have three parts to their bodies; head, thorax and abdomen and six legs. Spiders have two parts to their bodies and eight legs. The legs are attached to a combined head and thorax called the *cephalothorax,* not to the abdomen. Insects have two compound eyes and two *antennae* (feeling organs) and spiders normally have eight simple eyes and a pair of *palps* instead of antennae. Palps look and act like antennae, but they are also used when spiders mate.

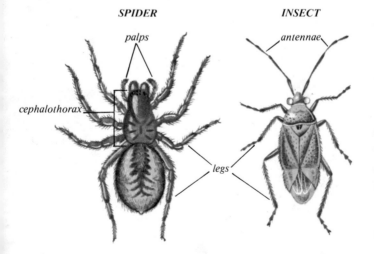

SPIDER   INSECT

palps   antennae

cephalothorax

legs

6   *Ciniflo fenestralis (10mm)*   *Tarnished plant bug*

The Abdomen

Detail of abdomen of Araneus quadratus (6-8mm)

Some spiders have very colourful bodies, especially the Green Spider, the Crab Spider and the Black Widow, while others are dull and drab.

The outside of a spider's body is surrounded by a relatively hard skin, the *integument,* which acts as an external skeleton and protects the soft insides of the spider from scrapes and bruises. Lots of fine hairs prevent water from reaching the integument, thus making the spider waterproof. Little bubbles of air trapped in the hairs act like a buffer between the skin and water when the spider falls in a pond or a puddle.

The abdomens of spiders found in Great Britain vary in size from about 2 cm across to some so small that you need a magnifying glass to see them. Exotic spiders in other countries have huge bodies in comparison, especially the well-known Bird-eating spider.

The Spinnerets

On the underside of the body, near the rear end, there are small organs called *spinnerets* which make delicate strands of silk for weaving webs and producing cushions or cocoons to wrap and protect the spider eggs. Spider silk is very fine and much better quality than the silk produced commercially in China by silk worms. Silk worms are the larvae of a moth called *Bombyx mori.* They are kept together in thousands, producing silk which the Chinese harvest for making expensive material. Spiders are not easy t keep together in large numbers because they have a tendency to attack and eat each other, which makes commercially impossible for anyone to set up a spide silk farm.

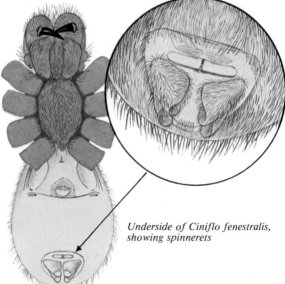

Underside of Ciniflo fenestralis, showing spinnerets

Spider movements

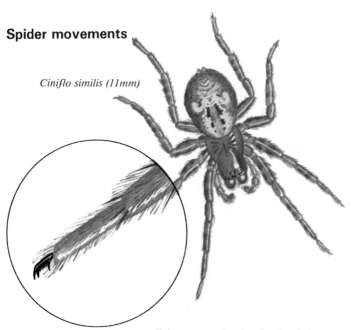

Ciniflo similis (11mm)

Enlargement, showing details of claw

The spider's eight legs are usually long, thin and wiry. The spider can run extremely fast and can move so quickly and so lightly that it can actually walk on water without getting wet. As the legs are very thin and springy they often get injured and broken when the spider is fighting, but it can grow new legs during the moulting period when the old skin is shed. A spider can run up walls and fences, and even walk upside down on ceilings and on the underside of leaves without slipping off. It can do this because of the shape of the claws on the end of each leg. The claws are also used for combing the silk produced by the spinnerets.

How spiders eat

Most kinds of spiders normally have eight eyes, but some have six. Generally they have poor eyesight and cannot see very far in front of them. Instead they rely on a very well-developed sense of touch in their palps which helps the spider to find its food. They are *carnivorous* (flesh-eaters) and they feed only on living creatures, especially moths, butterflies, flies, aphids, blackfly, thrips and lacewings.

Near the mouth of the spider is a pair of pincers called *chelicerae,* which contain the poison fangs. The

Pink Crab spider (5-7mm) traps a fly

spider uses these to nip its prey. The poison paralyses the struggling creature. The spider's mouth is too small to rip creatures such as butterflies and moths into small pieces for eating and so the spider either sucks the body juices from the prey, or uses the chelicerae and the palps to crush and liquefy it. With its fangs, the spider injects digestive juices into its prey to break it down before eating it.

Face of Crab spider,
Xysticus cristatus,
showing chelicerae

Small White butterfly

Lacewing

Aphids

The spider – hunter and victim

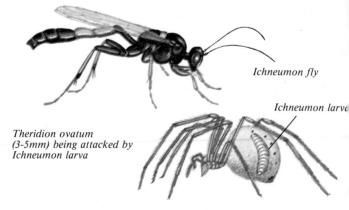

Ichneumon fly

Ichneumon larva

*Theridion ovatum
(3-5mm) being attacked by
Ichneumon larva*

Some spiders catch their food by using a silky trap
called a web, while others chase and pounce on insects
to make a kill. Even though we tend to be frightened
of them because of their quick, unpredictable
movements when they dart across the carpet, spiders
are a friend of Man because they kill millions of germ
spreading insects, such as flies. But spiders do have
their enemies. They are eaten by toads and frogs,
lizards and birds. Wrens in particular find that spiders
are very tasty, and use their sharp, slender beaks to
winkle them out of the cracks in wooden fences.
Ichneumon flies lay eggs on the backs of spiders.
When the flies' eggs hatch, the little grubs hang on,
slowly feeding off the unfortunate spider, eventually
killing it. These parasitic flies also lay their eggs inside
spider cocoons and the grubs eat all the spider eggs,
eventually wriggling out of the silky cocoon as adult
ichneumons. Spiders are sometimes their own worst

enemies. They are *cannibalistic,* which means they will eat each other, if given the chance.

Where are spiders found?

Spiders are found all over the world, sometimes in most unlikely places, such as swamps and deserts, on beaches on the coasts of the Indian Ocean, under Arctic snow fields and even at the top of Mount Everest.

Arachnologists have estimated that on a summer's day one could find as many as two million spiders living in an acre of grassland. Most of these would be the tiny black Money spider. Altogether there are 600 different kinds of spiders living in Great Britain. Most of them are solitary creatures, living alone for most of their life in nooks and crannies, waiting to catch some unsuspecting insect.

Money spider,
Linyphia triangulatis
(3-5mm), on web

Meadow grass

Sometimes the men who unpack cases of bananas shipped from overseas find frighteningly large, hairy spiders in the wooden packing cases, and quickly call in experts who take them to museums and zoos. People who search for fossils have discovered signs of spiders in rocks formed during the Devonian period, proving that spiders were living over 395 million years ago. Perfect specimens of spiders have been found preserved in Amber, formed around the Baltic Coast in the Oligocene Age, 38 million years ago, and these can be seen displayed in museum exhibitions.

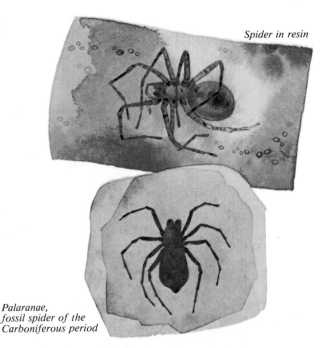

Spider in resin

*Palaranae,
fossil spider of the
Carboniferous period*

The spiders that we are most familiar with inside our homes are the long, thin, brown spiders that scurry around the inside of our baths, or can be seen lurking in cobwebs in neglected corners of kitchens and cupboards. There are several kinds of house spiders and all of them have long legs which help them to run quickly when danger, like the vacuum cleaner or dusting cloth, threatens! If left undisturbed, *Tegenaria* spiders will build huge webs shaped like sheets, up to a metre long, across the ceiling. But if the web is frequently disturbed, the spider gets discouraged and finds another place to spin its cobwebs to catch its food.

House spider,
Tegenaria domestica (10mm)

Of the house spiders, *Tegenaria parietina* has the longest legs and is often seen running under the furniture. This spider is also called the Cardinal spider. Legend has it that during the reign of Henry VIII, Cardinal Wolsey (1475-1530) was almost frightened to death one evening at Hampton Court, by a fierce looking spider in his bedroom. Since that time this long-legged spider has been called the Cardinal spider. Cardinal Wolsey's fear of spiders is shared by many children and adults. People who are disturbed and frightened by the quick, unpredictable and hurried movements of the spider suffer from a nervous condition called *Arachnophobia*.

Wolsey and the Cardinal spider, Tegenaria parietina (18mm)

Orb web of Meta segmentata (5-8mm)

Spiders in the garden

Our gardens are inhabited by large numbers of spiders, living and hunting on the ground, in the grass, amongst flowers, in bushes, garden sheds, trees and on fences. One of the biggest is the Garden or Diadem spider; the creature that spins the beautiful Orb web which looks so delicate and intricate when covered with dew or morning frost. In fact, the web is an efficient death-trap for other garden inhabitants.

Garden spider,
Araneus diadematus (12mm)

Crab spider,
Misumena ratia (10mm)

18

Crab spiders live among the garden flowers and are brightly coloured. The spider's colours blend with the plants, and it sits in the flower petals waiting to ambush a fly or moth. Crab spiders are well named because their front legs are longer than the others, and they walk like crabs.

One of the Green spiders, *Araneus cucurbitinus,* lives in apple trees and spins its web on the leaves, using the tips of the leaves as anchorage points. It is difficult to spot against the leaves, and is quite safe from wrens and sparrows hunting for some succulent spider to eat.

Araneus curcubitinus (5mm)

Another spider, *Dysdera,* feeds mainly on woodlice. It pierces the woodlouse between the joints with its fangs, and then uses its chelicerae to squeeze out the soft parts inside. This spider lives in greenhouses and conservatories where there are plenty of woodlice. Around the garden there are Wolf spiders hiding in holes in the ground, Jumping spiders that lie in the sun on fences and walls, and rare Spitting spiders lurking and waiting to spit at passing insects. Others have complicated names: *Meta segmentata* lives in dark shaded corners of the garden, while *Segestria senoculata* makes its home in walls and fences.

Dysdera crocata (10mm)

Theridion sisyphium (4mm)

The spider called *Theridion sisyphium* is the
commonest garden spider, but is one of the most
unusual because the female feeds its babies on little
pieces of flies. At first, the female spider feeds her
young with drops of liquid from her mouth, but later,
when a fly is caught, the mother spider uses her palps
and chelicerae to split the prey into small sections that
can be eaten by her spiderlings.

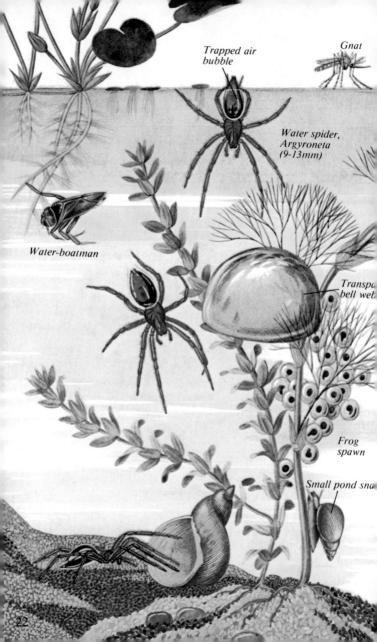

Trapped air bubble

Gnat

Water spider,
Argyroneta
(9-13mm)

Water-boatman

Transpa
bell web

Frog
spawn

Small pond sna

Mayfly nymph

Stickleback

The Water spider

One of the most interesting and unusual spiders is
the Water spider which spends most of its life under
water in ponds and canals. The female Water spider
spins a web close to some aquatic weed. The web is
shaped like a transparent bell. She fills it with air that
she brings down trapped between her hind legs. The
air bubbles are held close to her body by thousands of
fine hairs that cover the abdomen and legs of the
Water spider. She lives in the air-filled web, swimming
out from time to time to catch freshwater creatures
like beetle larvae and gnat larvae and brings them
back to her air-tent to eat. The male spider is bigger
than his mate which is unusual for spiders, and he
builds a web next to the female. He joins up the two
webs with a narrow tube and runs down the tube
when the time is right to mate with her.

How spiders catch their prey

As spiders feed entirely on small living creatures, they spend the biggest part of each day looking for something to eat. Although they are quite small it is not unusual for them to catch something bigger than themselves. Throughout the year all the spiders that live in our gardens kill huge amounts of garden pests for us, especially greenfly and blackfly which chew, suck and kill many garden crops. It has been said that without the spiders keeping down the fly population, we would soon be knee deep in flies and overrun with disease and pestilence.

All spiders paralyse their prey with poison by sinking their needle-sharp fangs into the victim's body. When they are ready to eat they pour digestive juices inside the limp and helpless creature, and then suck in all the body organs.

Some spiders, like the Black Widow which lives in America, can poison man and can even kill. None of our British species are dangerous. Most are too weak to get their fangs into our tough leathery skin, though the large house spider has strong fangs and its pincers can be felt if it gets a good grip on our skin.

Segestria senoculata (12-13mm)
paralyses Honey-bee

*Garden spider,
Araneus diadematus
(12mm), with Crane-fly
trapped in web*

Web-makers

Different types of spiders use different ways to
catch their food. Many spiders spin silky webs, which
is a method of catching food similar to the fisherman
netting fish at sea. The webs are positioned to catch
flying insects. They are very tough and sticky and
flying insects hit the trap and get stuck in the strands.
The trapped creature struggles in desperation to free
itself, but the more it struggles the more it gets
tangled in the web.

You can see lots of webs in the garden. The best
time to see the web in detail is on an early autumn
morning before the dew disappears, or after a sharp
frost. The drops of water stick to the silk strands and
glisten in the light from the sun like a string of tiny
diamonds. If you explore your garden at night with a
torch, many spiders can be discovered sitting and
waiting patiently in the middle of their intricate webs.
When the sun comes out in the morning the spiders
retreat and hide in the shade of a leaf or twig close to
the web.

Web-making

The web you will probably see in your garden is the large wagon-wheel shape called the Orb web, made by the Garden spider. The silk glands in the Garden spider's abdomen release liquid silk which hardens when it leaves the spinnerets. First the spider makes a geometric scaffolding. Then the spokes from the centre to the outside of the wheel are spun carefully into place by the spider. The spokes are dry and not sticky. Then threads of silk are woven from the centre around the spokes. The strands near the centre are damp and very sticky and these are the ones that catch the insects. Because the spider makes its web perhaps high up on a bush, it attaches a lifeline of silk to itself like a mountain climber attaches a rope. If a sharp breeze knocks the busy creature off, it swings for a moment, then clambers back again to carry on its work.

6

The trap is set

The web is soon ready. The spider hides close by on a leaf or a crack in a fence, and waits. When the victim is caught struggling in the web, the frantic movements of its wings and legs send vibrations up the lifeline to the spider. The spider climbs down the non-sticky thread, stabs the prey with its fangs, paralyses it and wraps it up carefully in a silk cocoon. When ready, the spider sucks out the inside of the creature, leaving the external skeleton of the victim to dangle in the breeze on a silky strand.

The webs are very elastic and tough, some are even strong enough to catch a bee. Although the effect of windy and rainy weather soon destroys them, the spiders can rebuild their complicated traps each morning as the whole process, from beginning to end, takes less than an hour.

Different webs

There are many different web patterns. The Hammock web is made by a spider that hangs upside down in the centre of the web waiting to feel the vibrations of a captured creature struggling to shake off the tangle of threads. The Cobweb or Sheetweb is made by the House spider. The *Amaurobius* spider makes an orb-shaped web without the centre platform. These small, untidy, circular webs with *Amaurobius* lurking behind are found in the dark corners of sheds and coalhouses and on the outside of holes in brick walls where the mortar has fallen out.

Garden spider's orb web

Hyptiotes trap snare

Money spider's hammock web

Purse web spider's tunnel

Segestria web

Amaurobius web

Wolf spider,
Lycosa tarsalis (6mm)

Jumping spider,
Salticus scenicus (7mm

Not all spiders build webs. Many are always on the prowl in the garden. They can outrun the creatures they are chasing and so they lie in ambush, hidden in holes or behind stones. The brown Wolf spider which is covered with long hairs, has good eyesight and can quickly spot anything moving close by. It can run faster than most of the.beetles in the garden, and after a struggle it kills the small prey with its poison fangs.

Crab spiders hide in flower petals and ambush their prey, while Jumping spiders, such as the black and white Zebra spider, stalk their food like a cat creeps after a bird, pouncing when they get near enough to use their fangs. The Spitting spider is a rare spider in England, and has six eyes not eight. It is an unusual hunter because it squirts a gummy substance from special glands in its body. Having pinned down its prey with this, the spider then saunters up to the trapped insect and bites with its fangs.

Greenbottle pinned down by gummy threads

Spitting spider, Scytodes (6mm)

The life cycle of the spider

As most spiders are short sighted, and will eagerly pounce on anything that comes close to them, courtship and mating is dangerous and sometimes fatal for the males which are normally smaller than the females. As the male spiders grow into adults they stop making webs and spend all their time in courtship with the females.

Since mating usually takes place on the female's web, the process is fraught with danger for the male. He has to get into the centre of the web, drumming a rhythm with his palps on the silken strands. This is to signal his interest in the female. There is a lifeline attached to his abdomen in case she gets nasty and frightens him off the web. The male spider is not easily put off and he will try and try again.

This characteristic determination was observed by the imprisoned Robert the Bruce in the 11th century. He was on the point of despair when he gained hope by watching a spider clambering up a single strand of silk to a female on a web high up on the ceiling. The spider kept falling, and trying again, and after many attempts eventually made it to the top.

Life cycle of the Garden spider, Araneus diadematus (12mm)

1   *Eggs are laid and wrapped in silky cocoon in Autumn*
2   *Developing eggs in Spring*
3   *Transparent spiderlings in hiding in May*
4   *Young spiders ready to disperse*
5   *Adult spider begins web making*

33

Mating

If the male spider convinces the female with his drumming that he is not a fly caught in the web, she will join him and mating takes place. He inserts a palp loaded with sperm into the female. Then he very quickly retreats from the female and the web. Quite often, he is unlucky and gets stuck in the threads, and ends up by being eaten. Mating takes place at different times of the year for different species but normally when the spider is reaching the end of its life.

Jumping spider, Salticus, waving palps

1 The male carries his own sperm in his palps and goes in search of a female. He often attaches a lifeline to himself to assist in a quick retreat.

He approaches cautiously on the female's web while she is eating something caught in the strands.

1　　*2*

Male and female Meta segmentata, mating — notice the female eating the trapped fly

34

The female leaves the web, finds a sheltered spot away from the wind and the rain, and lays her eggs. They are wrapped up in a thick protective cocoon made from silk. The eggs are the size of a pinhead and the cocoons look like little balls of cotton wool. You can see them hidden away in the knot holes in wooden fencing around the garden, on window sills, in ceiling corners and even on lumps of coal and coke in a coalhouse.

Egg sac

2 *Before mating, the male and female tap each other's legs.*

3 *When the male has been accepted, he embraces the female and places the sperm into her body using his palps.*

4 *He must then retreat quickly, otherwise he may be killed and eaten by the female.*

3

4

Egg to adult

As the eggs are very small, as many as 200 can fit into each cocoon. In many species of spiders the eggs remain in this state throughout the winter months, and if the mother spider has been careful in choosing where to lay them, the eggs will survive the cold weather and the dangers of an occasional mouse or bird searching for food.

These eggs hatch in the warmth of spring and can often be seen in fields and meadows as a dense mass of writhing, wriggling spiderlings, which will soon get hungry and start to nibble each other. To avoid this, each spiderling uses its spinnerets to produce a fine strand of silk that billows in the breeze. Eventually, rather like a kite, the small creature is lifted into the air. The spiderlings get carried in all directions to other parts of the countryside to begin new lives when the strands of silk break or the breeze subsides.

Birds are always on the lookout for something special to eat and will swoop hungrily on the migrating spiders. Because of their large numbers, many fortunately survive to grow into adult spiders in their newly found home. And so the cycle is complete, from spider to egg, egg to spiderling, from spiderling to spider.

Meta segmentata (5-8mm)

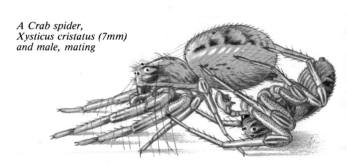

*A Crab spider,
Xysticus cristatus (7mm)
and male, mating*

Other spider mating habits

Crab spiders mate in another way. The male has a far better chance of survival than the web spider because he grabs the female's legs and holds her down with silky threads from his spinnerets so that she is unable to bite him during mating.

Jumping spiders and Wolf spiders dance in front of the females, showing off their body colours. The dance

*Wolf spider (5-6mm),
Lycosa*

*Jumping spider,
Salticus scenicus (7mm)*

*Wolf spider,
Lycosa (5-6mm),
carrying egg sac*

is an important mating signal, otherwise the female
may think the movement is a sign of food. The female
Wolf spider carries her eggs attached to her spinnerets.
The spiderlings climb onto her back when the eggs
hatch and she looks after them until they are big
enough to manage on their own.

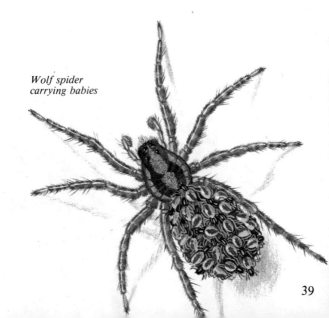

*Wolf spider
carrying babies*

Moulting

Young spiders grow very quickly and shed their skin
many times. This process is called *moulting*. If a leg is
broken in a tussle with a garden creature like a beetle,
a spider can grow a new one between moults. The
web-building spiders leave their old, but complete,
skins hanging on the web when they moult. If you
look closely at a Garden spider's web you could find a
shed skin dangling from a silken strand.

Moulting time is difficult for spiders and as it
happens eight or nine times throughout their life, not
all spiders survive. Feeding stops for a few days
beforehand and the creatures become very weak and
limp. Sometimes the spiders fail to remove themselves
completely and die in the struggle to get out of their
old skin.

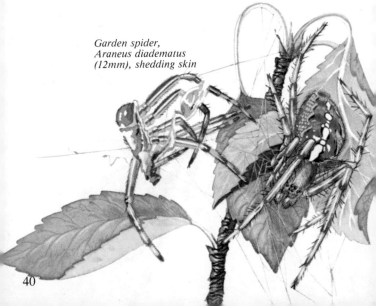

Garden spider,
Araneus diadematus
(12mm), shedding skin

Exotic spiders

Around the world, there are several large and frightening spiders that we would not want to find under our bedsheets. Most of the really big spiders live in countries which have warm and humid climates.

Ogre-faced spider, Dinopis (20mm)

lian spider, athema disippa mm)

Australian Red-backed spider (11-13mm)

Bird-eating spider, Theraphosid (5-7cm)

Tarantulas are perhaps the most well-known spiders, often being used by criminals in films and books to poison unsuspecting, sleeping victims. Tarantulas are not as big as people imagine. The abdomen measures about 2 cm. They do not spin webs, but like the British Wolf spider, catch their prey because of their speed. Tarantulas, unlike most British spiders, live in burrows, which they construct on dry and well-drained land. The burrows are lined with silk made by the spinnerets, making a dry and comfortable home.

Red-kneed spider, Brachyophelma smithi, from Mexico.
A Theraphosid often mistaken for a Tarantula

*Tarantula fabrilis (16mm),
very rare British Tarantula*

*Tarantula narbonensis (2.5cm),
at her burrow*

Giant Bird-eating spider

Bird-eating spiders are much bigger and often mistakenly called Tarantulas. They do not in fact eat birds, but they are big and vicious enough to hunt down and kill mice and voles with their fangs. They are more commonly found in South America, Australia and Africa.

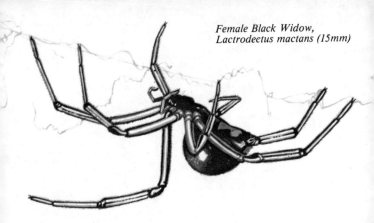

Black Widows and their numerous relatives live in America, Italy and South Africa. The Black Widow is well named, because the female kills the male after mating. It has a strong poison in its fangs which can kill a man and is considered one of the most dangerous of all the web-building spiders. The Black Widow is easily recognised by its black body with red markings on its underside and its dull and untidy web pattern.

Male and female
Black Widow spiders
mating

△ Sea spider, Pycnogonid,
length, including fully
extended legs, up to 40cm

▽ Raft spider,
Dolomedes triton (2.5cm)

The Marine or Sea spider inhabits the shores of the Indian and Pacific oceans. This spider prowls around the rock pools on the shoreline looking for small fish. Marine spiders can swim after their prey.

Another spider living close to water is the British Raft spider, *Dolomedes triton*. These spiders live in ponds and lakes and hunt their prey by running over the water to catch any insect landing on the water surface. This is one of the largest British spiders.

Australian Trap-door spiders have a unique way of catching their food. They dig small holes in the ground and cover the top with sticky soil particles. This acts like a trap-door and when something passes by, this spider leaps out, grabs the creature and pulls it into the hole. It then kills and eats it.

Trap-door spider

Scorpions, mites and ticks

Scorpions are also arachnids, easily recognisable because of their flexible tails with sharp stings at the end which contain poison glands. Like spiders, scorpions have four pairs of legs but also a pair of powerful pincers which are used for catching and holding prey before it is stung. Scorpions feed entirely upon animal food. They search for grasshoppers, beetles and other large insects, and occasionally will catch lizards and mice. The large pincers hold the prey and the scorpion brings its tail over its back and thrusts the sting into the struggling victim. Paralysis

Giant Black Jungle scorpion from Thailand

quickly follows, and the insect or animal is torn to pieces. The scorpion sucks the soft parts into its mouth.

Scorpions live in warm, tropical countries and make their homes under rocks and stones. They vary in size from about 2 cm to 20 cm in length. The strength and the amount of poison that a scorpion has depends upon the species. The poison can be so strong that it can kill a man unless treatment is given immediately.

Unlike spiders, scorpions are *viviparous* which means that the offspring are born alive and not as eggs. The young of a scorpion are born in two batches and are carried about on the mother scorpion's back until they are large and strong enough to look after themselves. The offspring look just like their parents and go through several moulting stages as they grow bigger.

Scorpion (2.5cm-20cm), carrying babies

Mites

Mites are very small arachnids and are found all over the world. They live on land, in fresh water streams, in ponds, marshes and the oceans. The largest species is about 1cm long and the smallest is invisible to the naked eye.

Many kinds of mites are *parasitic*. They feed on the blood of animals and birds. One species of mite is a great pest to chickens and pigeons. It sucks their blood and deprives them of sleep through constantly irritating their skin. Fresh water mites are generally coloured green or red and are easily identified in ponds and lakes. Their long legs are covered with hairs and are ideally shaped for swimming. Sea water mites are not good swimmers and spend their lives on the stems of seaweed.

Red poultry mite (1-2mm)

Harvest mites (1-3mm)

Flour mite (1-3mm)

Common house mite (1-3mm)

Ticks

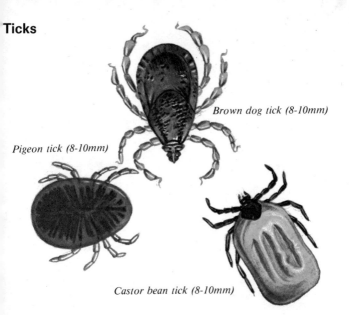

Brown dog tick (8-10mm)

Pigeon tick (8-10mm)

Castor bean tick (8-10mm)

Ticks are mites and are quite unpleasant creatures. They have very sharp teeth and suck the blood of other living creatures, even large mammals like cows, sheep and dogs. Many of them hang from branches and drop onto passing animals. They then crawl under the animal's fur and sink their jaws into its fleshy parts such as the neck or behind the ears. The ticks suck and fill up their own body with warm blood. Unlike spiders which do us so much good, ticks spread diseases. One, *Dermacentor reticulatus*, a tick living in North America, causes spotted fever in humans, an unpleasant disease that is common in towns in the Rocky Mountains where the tick occurs. Others can cause death in cattle, dogs, sheep, and even reptiles like snakes and lizards.

INDEX

All entries in italics denote illustrations only.
For specific species see Spiders.